STAR WARS

A VERY VADER VALENTINE'S DAY

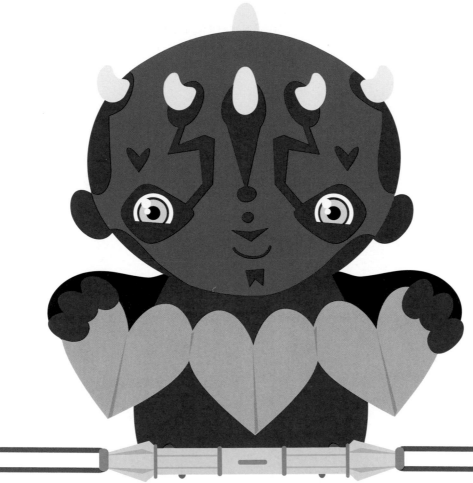

WRITTEN BY TREY KING   ILLUSTRATED BY KATIE COOK

ISBN 978-0-545-51560-3

12 11 10 9 8 7 6 5 4 3 2 1   13 14 15 16 17 18/0
PRINTED IN THE U.S.A.   138
FIRST PRINTING, JANUARY 2013

SCHOLASTIC INC.

A long time ago in a galaxy far, far away . . .

. . . IT WAS VALENTINE'S DAY!

There are many kinds of friends in the *Star Wars* universe—friends of all shapes, sizes, colors, and species. Whether you are a Jedi Master, a Sith Lord, an astromech droid, or a Hutt, the power of friendship is always your best ally!

R2-D2 & C-3PO

Everyone knows that the two best friends in the *Star Wars* galaxy are R2-D2 and C-3PO. These two droids have been friends for decades! R2-D2 had humble beginnings serving under Queen Padmé Amidala, while C-3PO was built by Anakin Skywalker. C-3PO would rather keep a safe distance from battle, but he always stays by the side of his spunky and adventurous friend R2-D2— even if that means following him into danger!

STAR WARS BEST FRIENDS

LUKE SKYWALKER & PRINCESS LEIA ORGANA

Luke grew up on a moisture farm in Tatooine. Far away, Leia grew up as a princess on Alderaan. When Luke saved Leia from a terrible fate on the Death Star, they became the best of friends. They both fought for the side of good in the Rebel Alliance, and eventually found out they were also brother and sister!

DARTH SIDIOUS & DARTH MAUL

"BFF" might not be the best way to describe Sidious and Maul, but it's a start. When Maul was just a baby, he was given to Sith Lord Darth Sidious, who trained him in the ways of the dark side of the Force. The two of them worked together to create all kinds of trouble for the Jedi.

ANAKIN SKYWALKER & PADMÉ AMIDALA

One is a Jedi Knight. The other is a Senator. But both Anakin and Padmé want peace for the galaxy—even if they disagree on how to get it. Despite their differences, they fell in love and got married. Anakin and Padmé were very happy together . . . until Anakin went to the dark side.

HAN SOLO & CHEWBACCA

Rebel hero Han Solo is best friends with his Wookiee copilot, Chewbacca. Aboard the *Millennium Falcon*, the two friends have gotten into all kinds of scrapes, but they always find a way out by working together! Their friendship can endure anything—even Han Solo's crush on Princess Leia.

JABBA THE HUTT & SALACIOUS CRUMB

Jabba Desilijic Tiure, better known as Jabba the Hutt, is the one of the galaxy's most ruthless gangsters! But where would he be without his not-so-loyal companion, Salacious B. Crumb? Salacious is a Kowakian monkey-lizard who works as Jabba's court jester. These two are a perfect pair because of their strange sense of humor and love of practical jokes.

JOKES!

What do you get if you mix a fruit with a bounty hunter?
Mango Fett!

Why did Han ask Chewie to copilot the *Millennium Falcon*?
Because he didn't like flying Solo.

What do you call five Sith Lords piled on top of a lightsaber?
A SITH KEBAB!

Where did Darth Maul get his facial markings?
At a Tatooine parlor.

Which side of an Ewok has the most hair?
The outside.

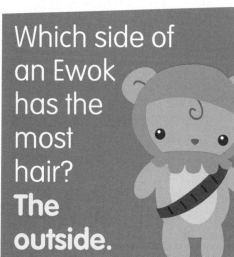

Where do Gungans store pickles?
In Jar Jars.

What do you get when you cross an elephant with Darth Vader?
An ele-vader.

Why should you never tell funny jokes on the *Millennium Falcon*?
Because the ship might crack up!

Why does Princess Leia wear buns on her head?
In case she gets hungry during a Senate meeting.

How does Queen Amidala congratulate herself?
With a Padmé on the back.

What happens when a red-and-white X-wing crashes into green Dagobah swamp water?
It gets wet.

Which *Star Wars* character works at a restaurant?
Darth Waiter.

Why do doctors make the best Jedi?
Because a Jedi must have patience.

Why is a droid mechanic never lonely?
Because he's always making new friends.

Why is Darth Maul still single?
Because he never found his other half.

Where does the Emperor go when he wants to buy something cheap?
He looks for a sale at the Maul.

Why did Darth Vader cross the road?
To get to the dark side.

Why was Chewbacca avoiding the princess?
Because he was afraid she might Leia kiss on him.

What time is it when an AT-AT steps on your chronometer?
Time to get a new chronometer.

Who tries to be a Jedi?
Obi-Wannabe.

CHOPSTICKS

SNACK FOR YODA

YUMMY

GAME TIME

WORD SEARCH

R2-D2 could use a little help finding some words. Can you help him out?

Hint: Words can be found going up and down and side to side.

WORDS:
- ANAKIN
- C3P0
- CLONE
- DROID
- EWOK
- FALCON
- FORCE
- HAN
- JEDI
- LUKE
- OBIWAN
- PADME
- PRINCESS
- R2D2
- SHIP
- SKYWALKER
- YODA

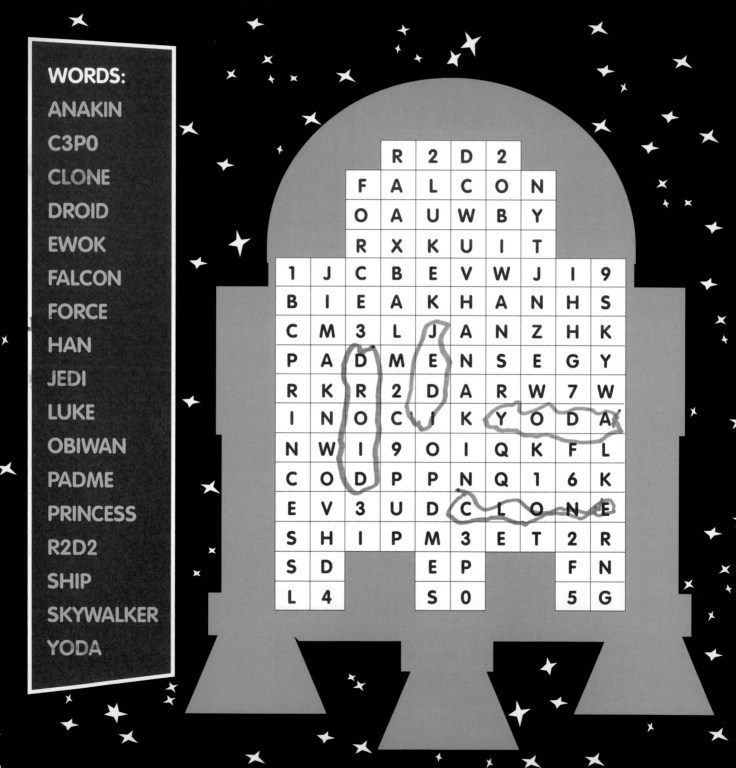

Word search grid letters (on sphere):

P D A R K S I D E C
P A O P D E N E N O
Q A R S H U N T E R U L
Q Z O T H C Y A D M Y I G
S I H C F E T T X J N H
P B H X Q T K O W Z A D T
A I V J H V R A L W O S
C R A B D W U H U C M A O A
E D E A T H S T A R K E B
I R S R G T K F M U J U R
H S T O R M L E L T G V
T R O O P E R F V U

WORDS:

COUNTDOOKU	HUNTER	SENATOR
DARKSIDE	HUTT	SITH
DARTHVADER	JAWA	SPACE
DEATHSTAR	LIGHTSABER	STORM
FETT	MAUL	TROOPER

YODA

Step 1

First, in pencil, lightly rough in the basic shape of the head and the body.

Step 2

Next, still in pencil, add the details of Yoda's arms, face, and clothing.

Step 3

Now, with a black pen or marker, trace over your pencil drawing. Erase your pencil lines!

Step 4

Using crayons or markers, color in your drawing!

DARTH MAUL

Step 1
First, in pencil, lightly rough in the basic shape of the head, horns, and facial features.

Step 2
Now, Darth Maul has lots of markings on his face. Using your pencil, draw in his tattoos.

Step 3
Next, with a black pen or marker, trace over your pencil lines. Erase your pencil lines. (Creepy, isn't he?)

Step 4
Lastly, use your crayons or markers to color in your artwork, and you're done!

Here's an activity that's fun to do on your own, or with a friend! Without looking at the next page, fill out the spaces below with your own favorite words. Then, use them to fill in the corresponding blanks on the next page. When you're done, you'll have made your very own silly *Star Wars* Valentine story!

1 ADJECTIVE _____

2 SCHOOL SUBJECT _____

3 ARTICLE OF CLOTHING _____

4 NOUN _____

5 VERB _____

6 ANIMAL _____

7 FOOD _____

8 NUMBER _____

9 COLOR _____

10 GAME _____

11 PLACE _____

12 SPORT _____

13 TOY _____

14 BODY PART _____

On Valentine's Day in a galaxy far, far away, there was a _____ Wookiee

1

named Chewbacca. He was having a bad day. Chewie was upset because he knew he

wouldn't do a good job on his _____ test. To make matters worse, Darth

2

Maul and Count Dooku had kicked mud onto Chewie's brand-new _____. By

3

the time Chewie got to school he was feeling sad.

But then Chewie's day started to turn around.

Queen Amidala gave him a _____ for Valentine's Day. He was so happy he

4

thought his head might _____. Luckily, it didn't. He had a Valentine's present for

5

her as well. He gave her a _____.

6

At lunch time, Chewie's best friend, Han Solo, shared his _____ with him.

7

Then their teacher Yoda brought the class Valentine's Day cupcakes. Everyone ate one,

except Chewie, who ate _____. Meanwhile, Jar Jar showed up with several

8

_____ Ewoks and they played _____.

9   **10**

Finally, the school bell rang and everyone got on the *Millennium Falcon* and flew to

_____ for a _____ match.

11   **12**

After several hours, they decided to have a party. Everyone was having a wonderful

time!

That is, until the Sith Lords showed up. Darth Maul kicked over the table, and Count

Dooku broke the radio. Everyone was upset. But Yoda remained calm as he approached

the evil-doers.

"In such a bad mood, you two are. Why?" he asked.

"Because no one gave me a(n) _____ for Valentine's Day," Count Dooku

13

said.

"Mine, you can have," Yoda offered.

Dooku was pleased with his gift and sat down to play with it.

Darth Maul was still fussy, until Queen Amidala gave him a small kiss on

his _____. Dooku and Maul were so happy, they used the Force to make Yoda

14

and Chewie fly into the air in celebration!

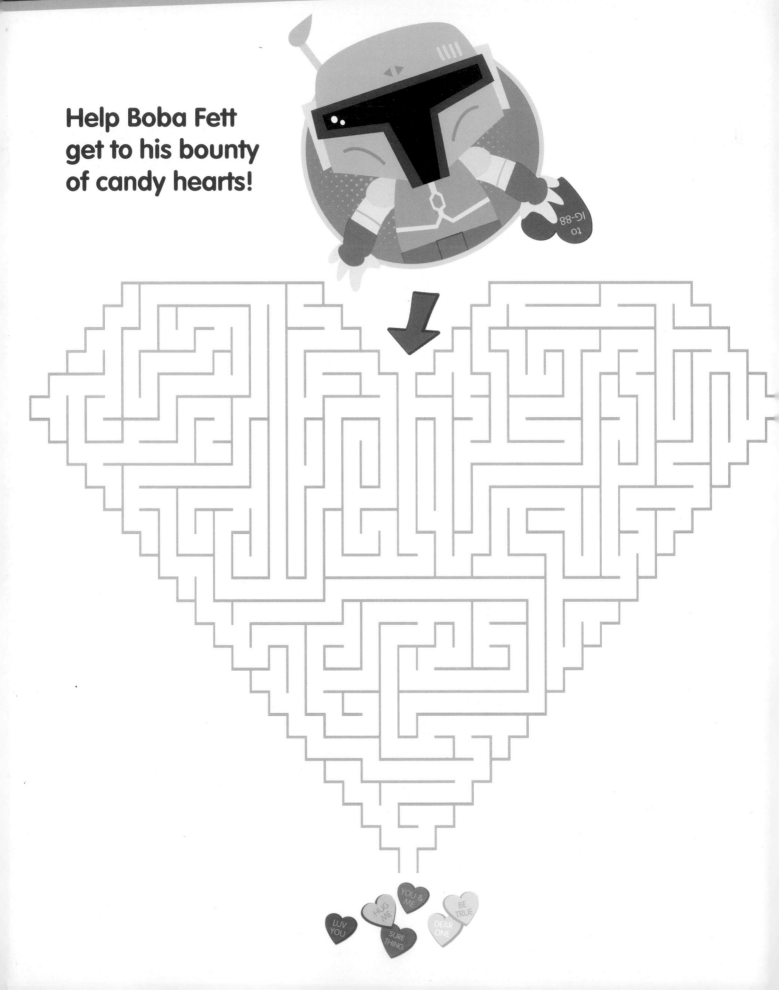

Help Boba Fett get to his bounty of candy hearts!

TO:

FROM:

© 2013 LUCASFILM LTD. & TM.

TO:

FROM:

© 2013 LUCASFILM LTD. & TM.

TO:

FROM:

© 2013 LUCASFILM LTD. & TM.

TO:

FROM:

© 2013 LUCASFILM LTD. & TM.

TO:

FROM:

© 2013 LUCASFILM LTD. & TM.

TO:

FROM:

© 2013 LUCASFILM LTD. & TM.

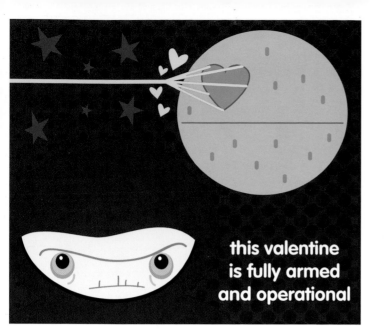

TO:

FROM:

© 2013 LUCASFILM LTD. & TM.

TO:

FROM:

© 2013 LUCASFILM LTD. & TM.

TO:

FROM:

© 2013 LUCASFILM LTD. & TM.

TO:

FROM:

© 2013 LUCASFILM LTD. & TM.

TO:

FROM:

© 2013 LUCASFILM LTD. & TM.

TO:

FROM:

© 2013 LUCASFILM LTD. & TM.

I really OBI-WAN you to be my VALENTINE

You're my only hope... ...for a Happy Valentine's Day!

Valentine, don't make me spend the day SOLO

THE FORCE IS STRONG WITH YOU, VALENTINE

OUR LOVE WILL ENDOR

YOU HOLD THE WOO-KEY TO MY HEART

TO:

FROM:

© 2013 LUCASFILM LTD. & TM.

TO:

FROM:

© 2013 LUCASFILM LTD. & TM.

TO:

FROM:

© 2013 LUCASFILM LTD. & TM.

TO:

FROM:

© 2013 LUCASFILM LTD. & TM.

TO:

FROM:

© 2013 LUCASFILM LTD. & TM.

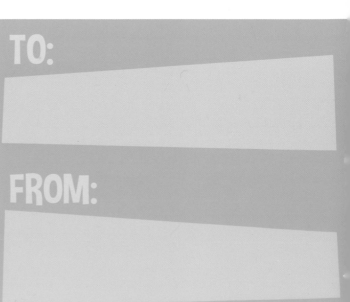

TO:

FROM:

© 2013 LUCASFILM LTD. & TM.